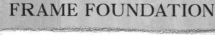

FRAME FOUNDATION

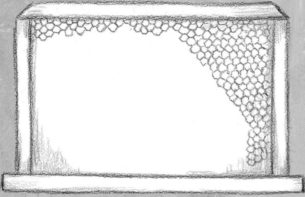

A frame foundation is a sheet of plastic coated with wax that's impressed with a honeycomb pattern. It helps bees get their own honeycomb started.

BEEHIVE

Beekeepers take honey from here.

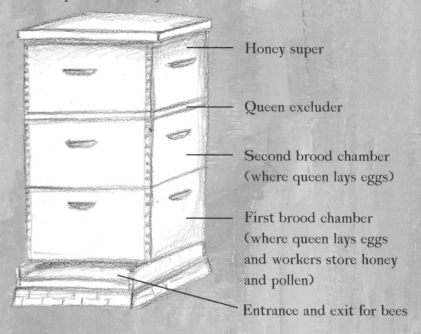

Honey super

Queen excluder

Second brood chamber (where queen lays eggs)

First brood chamber (where queen lays eggs and workers store honey and pollen)

Entrance and exit for bees

WAGGLE DANCE

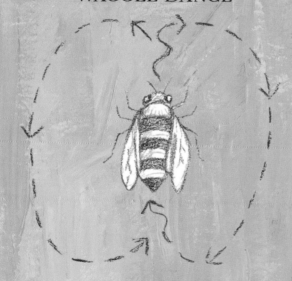

This dance lets other workers know where they can find flowers. The direction in which the bee moves tells where the flowers are in relation to the sun. The time the waggle lasts tells how far away the flowers are.

BEEHIVE SECTIONAL

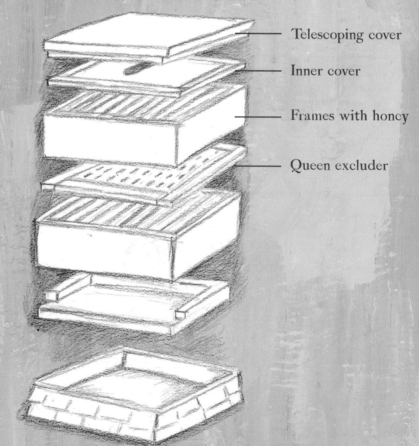

Telescoping cover

Inner cover

Frames with honey

Queen excluder

Library of Congress Cataloging-in-Publication Data
Nargi, Lela. The honeybee man / Lela Nargi; illustrated by Kyrsten Brooker.—1st ed. · p. cm. · Summary: Fred, a beekeeper whose hives are on the roof of his Brooklyn, New York, apartment building, tends his bees and distributes their honey to his neighbors. Includes facts about bees and beekeepers. ISBN 978-0-375-84980-0 (trade) — ISBN 978-0-375-95695-9 (glb) [1. Honeybee—Fiction. 2. Bees—Fiction. 3. Beekeepers—Fiction. 4. Bee culture—Fiction.] I. Brooker, Kyrsten, ill. II. Title. PZ7.N162Br 2011 · [E]—dc22 · 2009044216

The text of this book is set in Minion.
The illustrations were rendered in collage and oil paint.
Book design by Rachael Cole

MANUFACTURED IN MALAYSIA
10 9 8 7 6 5 4 3 2 1
First Edition

For Ada, my own
flower-loving bee.
—L.N.

In memory of my
grandparents, Cecil
and Irene Fargey.
—K.B.

The Honeybee Man

by Lela Nargi

pictures by Kyrsten Brooker

schwartz & wade books · new york

One quiet July dawn, Fred rolls out of his bed and into his slippers. He greets two members of his enormous family:

   "Good morning, Copper!" he calls to his dog, still curled up on the rug.

   "Good morning, Cat," he calls to his cat named Cat. She stretches in a pool of sunlight.

Fred shuffles downstairs to the kitchen and fixes a
cup of tea. He takes his teacup in one hand and creaks
back upstairs, then up another flight. Climbing a ladder
that climbs the wall, he pushes open a hatch and pulls
himself out onto the roof.

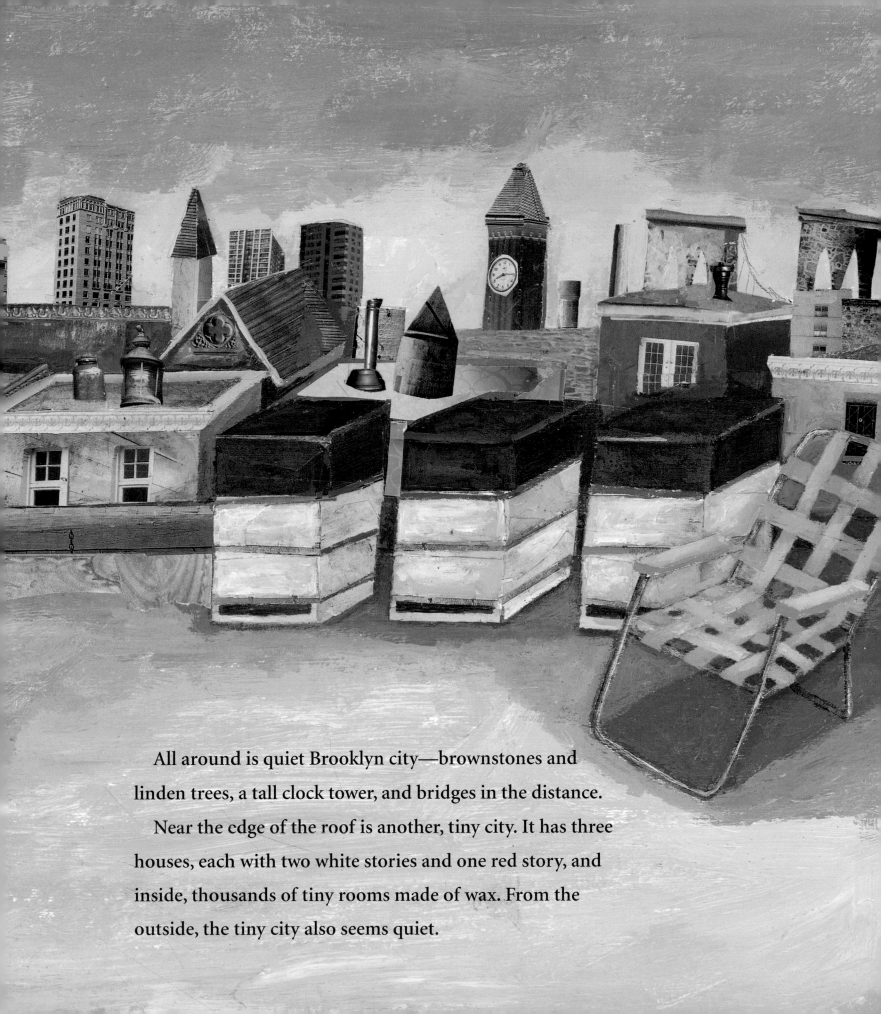

All around is quiet Brooklyn city—brownstones and linden trees, a tall clock tower, and bridges in the distance.

Near the edge of the roof is another, tiny city. It has three houses, each with two white stories and one red story, and inside, thousands of tiny rooms made of wax. From the outside, the tiny city also seems quiet.

Fred inhales the smells of a summer city morning:
maple leaves and gasoline and the river and dust.
He turns to the tiny city and inhales its smaller,
sweeter smell—a little like caramel,
a little like ripe peaches.

To the first little house Fred calls,
"Good morning, Queen Mab."

And to the other two houses,
"Good morning, Queen Nefertiti.
Good morning, Queen Boadicea."

Then Fred greets the rest
of his family, which has more
members than he can count:
"Good morning, my bees,
my darlings!"

Inside their houses, the three queen bees and their thousands of worker bee daughters don't answer. But Fred knows they are busy. The queens are laying eggs. Some workers are building wax rooms, some are feeding babies, some are making the hive tidy. Others are getting ready to forage in flowers abloom all across Brooklyn.

Fred closes his eyes and lets his mind wander. Will Queen Mab's daughters find mint flowers, as they did last year? Will Queen Boadicea's honey be dark like molasses, or light and clear like amber?

As he thinks about honey, Fred's mouth begins to water. "I can't wait to find out!"

Fred pictures the park at the end of his block. He imagines his bees moving from clover to clover, flying over them low and slow with their see-through wings, which flap and also twist like propellers. Fred wishes he could fly there with them, with the wind rushing over his back.

Fred opens his eyes and the hives are alive, humming with a low hum, as low as a whisper. Fred hums back,

"Tell me what it's like to fly through the world!"

Zzzzzz! hum the bees. To Fred, this sounds like an answer. If only he could understand!

Young bees on their first flights circle in the air.

"There, there, my girls. Don't be afraid!" Fred says in a soothing voice. As he speaks, the young bees seem to pluck up their courage. On the streets below, trucks rumble and babies wail in their strollers. But inch by inch the young bees shimmy past the edge of their tiny city.

It is easy for Fred to recognize the older bees, who are used to moving between their small world and the giant world of people. They zip out of the hives and throw themselves at the air, embracing it with their wings. A few land on Fred's arms.

"Hello, Fred!" they seem to say.

"Hello, girls. Have a nice day. Now off you go!" Fred gives them a gentle flick with a finger and away they *Zzzzz!*

Fred watches his bees fly into his backyard garden and other gardens on the block. He sees the bees dive into sweet pea and squash flowers. If he were closer, he could see them using their tubelike tongues to drink in flower nectar, which they store in honey sacs inside their bellies. Then it's off to the next pea plant, to the sage flowers in the next backyard, and maybe, if Fred is lucky, to blooming blueberry bushes somewhere across town.

When the bees return to their hives, Fred notices that they are flying *s l o o o w l y*—heavy, now, with nectar.

Inside, Fred knows they are performing waggle dances to tell the others where the best flowers grow.

He knows that sister bees are taking the nectar and storing it in the tiny wax rooms.

And he knows that others are fanning their wings to evaporate the water from the nectar so it will turn to honey.

Day after day Fred watches the bees zip out over the blare of the city.

"How tireless you are," he sighs, wishing he could be as strong and as free as the bees.

One afternoon at the end of August, Fred climbs again to his roof. He is wearing his black rubber rain boots and his white head veil and a scratch on his hand from Cat the cat, who did not want to be woken this morning. He makes an announcement to the bees:

"Sweeties, I have come for the honey."

And a plea:

"Please do not sting me!"

Fred puffs clouds of smoke into the tiny houses, and the bees burrow deep down into the hive.

From the very top floor, Fred lifts out the honeycomb. He packs it into buckets and says,
"Thank you for this honey, bees."
Zzzzz!

Fred hauls the buckets down the ladder and into his house, where he banishes Copper the honey-loving dog to the kitchen.

Fred sets a frame of honeycomb over a plastic tank and slices off the wax caps, and the honey begins to flow.

He places the honeycomb in a spinning machine, which squeezes every last drip of honey out of it.

He pours the honey into jars.

Then he sticks labels to the jars: FRED'S BROOKLYN HONEY, MADE BY TIRELESS BROOKLYN BEES.

In the late afternoon, Fred sits on his
stoop, enjoying the cool end-of-summer
breeze. When his neighbors come out
to chat, Fred gives each of them a jar of
deep gold honey.

One neighbor asks, "Where did this honey come from?"
And Fred says, in a humming sort of whisper,
"From the sweet pea flowers in your backyard. From
the flowers of the linden trees shading our block. And
maybe, if we are *lucky,* from sour-sweet blueberry bushes
somewhere across town."

Up on Fred's roof,
the bees are huddled back in their
own city, waiting for the rays of tomorrow's
sun to call them up and away over Brooklyn.
Their wings are tattered from flying, and the nip of
autumn is in the air. Soon it will be time to rest.

Down on the stoop, Fred opens a jar of honey. The honey glistens
and shimmers in the last of the sunlight. Fred sticks in a finger.

It is sweet, like linden flowers.

It is sharp, like rosemary.

It is ever-so-slightly sour.

"Ah," says Fred, absorbing these happy flavors. "Blueberries!"

Some Amazing Facts About Honey, Honeybees, and Beekeepers

People like Fred, who keep bees so they can collect (and eat!) their honey, are called beekeepers, or apiarists. Fred's story is inspired by two Brooklyn, New York, *apiarists,* one of whom has been beekeeping in his Fort Greene neighborhood since 2001.

Beekeepers take care of groups of honeybees, called *colonies.* Each colony lives in its own bee house, called a *hive.* Some hives are gentle, some are cranky; some make lots of honey, some make less.

Each hive has one queen, whose only job is to lay eggs—up to fifteen hundred a day. Fred names his bees after queens from history and folklore: Nefertiti was the wife of the Egyptian pharaoh Akhenaton; Mab is a fairy queen of Celtic legend; and Boadicea was a real Celtic queen who led a rebellion against soldiers of the Roman Empire.

Each hive has several hundred male *drones,* whose only job is to mate with the queen. The rest of the bees in a colony are female workers, and they are all sisters. In summer, when the colony is foraging, there can be as many as sixty thousand workers in a hive; in winter, as few as ten thousand. In their first phases of life, they feed the queen and the *brood* (eggs, larvae, pupae—these are all stages of baby bee–hood). They build six-sided wax rooms, or *cells,* on wooden frames that the beekeeper places inside the hive, which hold nectar, pollen and honey; this is called *honeycomb.* The workers also keep the hive clean and perform many other tasks. When they are about fourteen days old, they fly out to forage for flower nectar.

When a bee finds a plentiful crop of flowers, she tells the other bees about it with a *waggle dance*. This shows how far from the hive, and in what direction in relation to the sun, the flowers lie. In one day, a honeybee may travel eight miles and visit a thousand flowers—and still, in her lifetime of about twelve weeks, she will collect enough nectar to make only a twelfth of a teaspoon of honey!

In late summer or early autumn, the honeycomb is full of honey and ready for harvest. Beekeepers burn kindling, like pine needles, and puff the smoke into the hive. This makes the bees think there is a fire, and they scramble to eat as much honey as they can to prepare for their escape. They are too busy to care what the beekeeper is doing. The beekeeper takes honeycomb *only* from the top *super,* or level, of the hive. The honeycomb in the lower supers he leaves for the bees—the honey there is their food for the winter.

The beekeeper removes the honey from the honeycomb with a spinning machine called an *extractor* and pours it into jars for us to enjoy . . . maybe forever! Traces of still-edible honey have been found in the tombs of Egyptian pharaohs.

By the end of October, most of the bees have left the hive to die. The queen—who has a life span of about three years—and workers born in autumn live out the winter huddled close on top of the honeycomb for warmth. They move from one honey-filled segment to the next, eating and resting and, if bees can dream, dreaming of a brand-new spring.

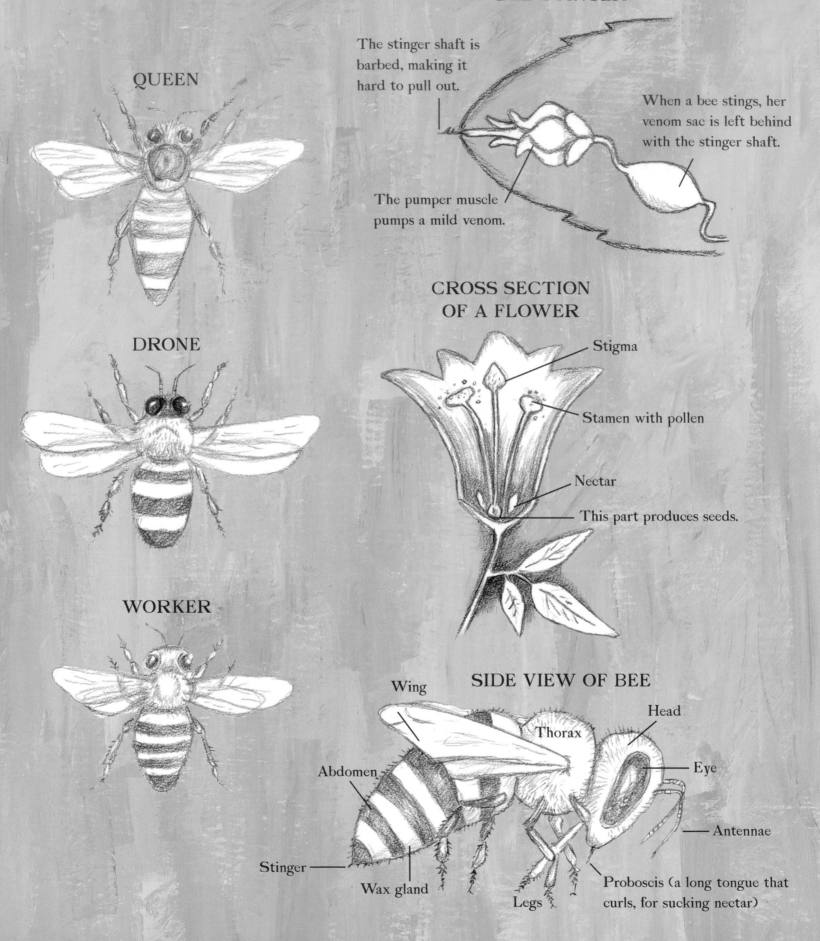

QUEEN

DRONE

WORKER

BEE STINGER

The stinger shaft is barbed, making it hard to pull out.

When a bee stings, her venom sac is left behind with the stinger shaft.

The pumper muscle pumps a mild venom.

CROSS SECTION OF A FLOWER

Stigma

Stamen with pollen

Nectar

This part produces seeds.

SIDE VIEW OF BEE

Wing

Head

Thorax

Abdomen

Eye

Stinger

Antennae

Wax gland

Legs

Proboscis (a long tongue that curls, for sucking nectar)